PIGGIES
in the KITCHEN

MICHELLE MEADOWS   ILLUSTRATED BY ARD HOYT

Simon & Schuster Books for Young Readers New York London Toronto Sydney

Little snouts and curly tails,
pink feet jumping high.
Hugs and kisses all around,
Mama says, "Good-bye."

Piggies in the kitchen,
climb up to the top.
Dig through all the cupboards—
careful not to drop!

Squeeze out sticks of butter,
flour in the bowl.
Carton takes a tumble,
eggs begin to roll.

GLUP, GLUP,
OINK, OINK—Pour another cup.

VROOM, VROOM, VROOM, VROOM—

"Someone's driving up!"

Cover up the batter,
hide the wooden spoon.
Brush away the sugar,
whistling a tune.

SNIP, SNAP go the blinds.
"Is Mama coming NOW?"

"Nope, it isn't Mama!
It's only Mrs. Cow."

Piggies in the kitchen,
sprinkle chocolate chips.
Two sneak the frosting,
and one piggy drips.

SWISH, SWISH, OINK, OINK—
Stir it to the beat.

VROOM, VROOM,
VROOM,
VROOM—
"Someone's in
the street!"

Cover up the batter,
hide the wooden spoon.
Brush away the sugar,
whistling a tune.

SNIP, SNAP go the blinds.
"Who's outside the house?"

"Nope, it isn't Mama!
It's only Mrs. Mouse."

Piggies in the kitchen,
roll the dough across.
Add cinnamon and
whipped cream,
pour the chocolate sauce.

TWIST, TWIST, OINK, OINK—

Open up the jar.

VROOM, VROOM, VROOM, VROOM—

Piggies holler, "CAR!"

Cover up the batter,
hide the wooden spoon.
Brush away the sugar,
whistling a tune.

SNIP, SNAP go the blinds.
BEEP, BEEP, BEEP—
"Nope, it isn't Mama!
It's only Mrs. Sheep."

Piggies in the kitchen,
wipe off baby's dress.
Papa yells, "Oh, no!
Who made such a mess?!"

"C'mon, Papa, help us.
Turn the oven high."

"Don't forget the pie!"

DING, DING, DING, DING—Take the goodies out.

SNIFF, SNIFF, OINK, OINK— Watch your little snout.

Mama's really coming.
Baby piggy's stuck.

STOMP,
STOMP,
STOMP,
STOMP—

"Everybody, duck!"

Mama's in the kitchen.
She can't believe her eyes.

POP,
POP,
POP,
POP—

What a pig surprise!

"Happy Birthday, Mama!
We love you!"

For Chase, my favorite piggy—M. M.

To my baby sister, Shannon, who was always as pretty as a picture,
but played like one of the boys! I love you so—A. H.

ACKNOWLEDGMENTS
With special thanks to Julia Maguire and Kevin Lewis.—M. M.

SIMON & SCHUSTER BOOKS FOR YOUNG READERS

An imprint of Simon & Schuster Children's Publishing Division · 1230 Avenue of the Americas, New York, New York 10020

Text copyright © 2011 by Michelle Meadows · Illustrations copyright © 2011 by Ard Hoyt

All rights reserved, including the right of reproduction in whole or in part in any form.

SIMON & SCHUSTER BOOKS FOR YOUNG READERS is a trademark of Simon & Schuster, Inc.

For information about special discounts for bulk purchases, please contact Simon & Schuster Special Sales at 1-866-506-1949 or
business@simonandschuster.com. · The Simon & Schuster Speakers Bureau can bring authors to your live event. For more information
or to book an event, contact the Simon & Schuster Speakers Bureau at 1-866-248-3049 or visit our website at www.simonspeakers.com.

Book design by Jessica Handelman · The text for this book is set in Bembo Infant.

The illustrations for this book are rendered in pen and ink with watercolor on Arches paper. · Manufactured in China

1110 SCP

2 4 6 8 10 9 7 5 3 1

CIP data for this book is available from the Library of Congress.

ISBN 978-1-4169-3787-6